ADVANCE PRAISE FOR HER
UPCOMING NOVEL, BLUE WOMAN
BURNING

Haunting and dreamlike, *Blue Woman Burning* takes us on an unforgettable journey through a broken family's hidden past and one woman's struggle to transcend it.

~Erika Schickel, author, *The Big Hurt* and *You're Not the Boss of Me*

Blue Woman Burning is magical realism at its best. When Fallon's mother vanishes in the desert one day, it sends her on a heartbreakingly beautiful quest to understand the mysteries of life, and of her own family. This is an inspiring coming-of-age story with a smash bang ending you won't see coming."

~Matt Witten, writer for the TV series, HOUSE and bestselling author of *The Necklace*

Imagine a collaboration between Madeleine L'Engle and Carlos Castaneda and you'll have some idea of Lâle Davidson's *Blue Woman Burning*. It's a contemporary quest novel with mythic echoes, a mystery with lashings of the supernatural, a road trip in search of family, romance, and magic. Enthralling!

~Steve Stern, award-winning author of *The Angel of Forgetfulness*

Skip the acid. For a rush of transmogrification, read this novel. Lâle Davidson writes more authentically about crazy suffering than most anyone I've read. And she writes it with a voice so clean and astringent we have no trouble believing the unbelievable. Her voice is beautiful, no-nonsense, ferociously informed. Terrific.

~Bob Miner, author of *Mother's Day* and *Exes*

Lâle Davidson's *Blue Woman Burning* is at once a road novel, a mystery, and a wise meditation on family and the way hurt begets hurt. As propulsive as its plot is, though, it's Davidson's wondrous, penetrating, eloquent prose that will stick with readers. This book is that rare thing: a page-turner that can and should be savored.

~Gabriel Blackwell, author of *Correction* and editor of *The Rupture*

STRANGE APPETITES

LÂLE DAVIDSON

Strange Appetites

Copyright © 2021 by Lâle Davidson

All rights reserved

Published by Red Penguin Books

Cover illustration by Penny Weber

Bellerose Village, New York

Library of Congress Control Number: 2021921774

ISBN

Print 978-1-63777-168-6

Digital 978-1-63777-167-9

Love and thanks to Charley, Tess,
the WMDs, and SUAWP

CONTENTS

Something there is that doesn't love a wall,
That sends the frozen-ground-swell under it,
And spills the upper boulders in the sun;
And makes gaps even two can pass abreast.

"Mending Wall," Robert Frost

THE OPAL MAKER

When they cracked my sister's ribs open and slid the curved bone blades back under her skin to repair her damaged heart, they found me tucked inside. Up until then, I had not known how her ribs cradle-gouged me.

The head surgeon was Russian, so nothing much surprised him. "It happens more often than you would think," he said. "One of her valves ripped because it was pumping blood for two instead of one." As he spoke, his left eye drilled into me, black and shiny as the word *one*.

You might think it's hard to breathe when you're living inside someone else. It is. But surprisingly, you adjust. Your mind goes hazy, your hearing muted. You close your eyes and lie still, warm, and bound. You grow to love being bound. You attune yourself to the other's heartbeat, the gurgling stomach, the burbling sounds from outside that muzzy your ears until you forget there ever was an outside. Sounds shine in your mind like light through stained glass. Such bright colors! How they bloom and swirl. You grow to love, love, love this body to the exclusion of your own. You press and probe and drill and wind yourself into every tiny space it affords until you are ripping it apart at the same time you are holding it together.

So, I can't say I was glad when they pulled me out. Not at all. I hadn't developed very far, my limbs flat and folded in on themselves, a plant caught under a stone, my skin opaque, ridged as a water-logged lizard. Light pierced my cranium forcing my eyes open, raw as wounds. Air sanded my skin, and cold moved in like the enemy.

They peeled me out, repaired her torn valve, slid her ribs back in place, and stitched her up. If she felt empty inside, she didn't say. She went back to her job of sorting gemstones, and I became useless. I couldn't walk, couldn't feed myself, couldn't think my own thoughts. The bright lights in my mind went out, and what I found there instead were mushrooms.

For a long time after they took me out, all I could think about was snipping those stitches and crawling back in. In fact, that was how I learned to walk again, by flopping onto the floor as soon as she went to bed, and pressing my arms and knees against the ground until my muscles grew fiber that could hold me up. At first, my fingers flew haphazardly as I twisted them through the scissor handles, but eventually they began to obey my thoughts, and I marveled at how the twin blades opened and then, by pressing themselves against each other, delineated an edge, the power of separation a revelation.

In darkness, since I didn't need light to see, I hunched over her sleeping form and pulled back the covers as soundlessly and deftly as I had moved inside her. But to my shock, her flesh had knitted itself back together. It had taken me too long to get there. The scar gleamed in the moonlight, a talisman of individuation, a shield, closing me out of her forever.

I was devastated.

But I was standing.

What a miracle of balance standing was, my muscles, mind, bone and sinew, even my back, that magnificent, curved snake with its tiny tail wagging between my hips, all adjusting and attuning to each other, speaking their own tiny words, a minute orchestration of falling and pushing back, teetering and balancing, letting go and holding on.

I dropped the scissors and stepped out into the garden, flowers glowing in moonlight. Scent was another discovery, so much information feathering your lungs, igniting memories. I inhaled and exhaled, again and again, loving how I could stroke myself on the inside simply by breathing. With my skin now smooth and toughened, the air felt like another soft body enveloping me, but this body allowed me to move whichever way I willed.

That's when she began to hate me.

She didn't say it, but I could feel it in her gray eyes the next morning, her freckled skin, the way her mind went blank whenever she sat across from me as if I wasn't worth even thinking thoughts about, and the way she hid the gems she was sorting whenever I entered the room. After those first giant steps, my progress slowed to torturously small increments, so I grew more frustrated. And whenever I cried, she would reach for her own throat to strangle it off. I would have to dig my nails between her clenched fingers and white throat to peel them away or else watch her sputter and choke. The night I awoke to find her hands around my own throat, I left.

Do I miss her? Yes. Do I sometimes wish that someone else would live my life for me? Who wouldn't?

But, ah, the smell of sunshine on a dusty sidewalk in spring, of flowers in cats' fur. And sound! Tire tread on pavement and laughter of children flow into the skull as cool and crisp as water.

Now I sit on a street corner in the busy part of town. People bring me their stories and fragments of thought. I cup the sounds in my hands, and if I press my palms together hard enough between my thighs, the sounds turn into opals, not perfectly round, a little oblong and misshapen, but silky smooth and shining with interior light. They swallow the opals, and colors shine from their eyes. Then for just a moment, I feel connected to them and we all become light, illuminating each other.

DIVORCE IN A NEW LIGHT

As I sat in the doctor's office, waiting for my daughter to come out of her appointment, an elderly gentleman struck up a conversation with me. He had steady eyes, an easy smile, and a knack for storytelling.

This is what he told me.

After fifty years of marriage, his wife announced over breakfast, "Larry, I want a divorce." Then she spooned the last bit of soft-boiled egg into her mouth, the egg he had made for her.

The coffee cup stopped midway to his mouth. "A divorce."

"Yes." She pressed her gums together, collapsing her lips inward. She hadn't bothered to put in her dentures that morning. The sunlight gleamed off the two little hairs that grew out of the bottom of her chin.

"Why would you want a divorce? Divorce is for unhappy people. We're happy. We love each other." He gestured as if folding their surroundings into an egg-white soufflé.

"I want to learn who I really am," she replied, replacing her spoon on the table and pressing it into place for emphasis.

"But you know who you are. You're you. Always have been."
Again, with the hands.

"No, I don't."

"You don't?" His cheeks puffed out and he leaned forward.

"No. I've always been your wife. Larry's wife. We married too young, Larry. I want to live on my own. Explore myself before I die."

"So? Go explore yourself." He flicked his fingers in an off-you-go gesture. "I'm not stopping you."

"I just can't be myself around you."

"What do you mean? You pee with the door open. I know what your morning breath smells like. If that's not intimacy, I'm a silver teapot."

"You know what I mean."

"No, I don't."

"I mean, I'm too dependent on you. I've never done anything by myself. I need to be in charge of myself."

"Well, if you want to be in charge, be in charge. I don't mind. You boil the egg next time. You drive the car. I don't need to be in charge."

"That's not what I mean."

"What do you mean?"

"I want a divorce."

"Okay, then." He set the coffee cup down. "I love you. I'll give you a divorce."

"Good. When can we do it?"

"Call Harry. Set up an appointment."

"Good. Would you make the call?"

"Of course."

"I have a haircutting appointment today. Can you drive me there?"

"Anywhere you want to go. You're in charge."

Just then my daughter came out of the doctor's office.

"We've been divorced for six months now," he finished.

"I'm sorry," I said.

He smiled. "All things considered, divorce isn't that bad. I have to drive her around a lot more to do her errands. But I enjoy that."

His wife came out of another doctor's office, then, a bent woman in a flowered dress. He stood, waved goodbye to me, and offered her his arm. They shuffled carefully out of the office.

From the hall, I heard him say, "Where to next, my dear?"

MY SISTER'S LABYRINTH

By the time I found my second sister, she had built a wall around her house that obscured its stained-glass windows. I circled and circled, and finally found an opening hidden by a rose bush trained to the wall by many ties. The opening led into a boxwood labyrinth where, at intervals, gardens bloomed. For twenty years I walked the labyrinth, trying to get to her house.

When I finally found her front door, I knocked. She answered, her brows pursed in concentration, the lines around her mouth squared.

"It is so hard for me when family visits," she said, "because my boundaries are so thin."

I pondered this. "Let's at least have lunch before I go."

"I require an appointment. I have a husband and three children and will have to see where I can fit you in."

The path to the street turned out to be only a few short steps from her door.

She met me at a café three days later. When I hugged her, my arms—expecting to find the resistance of flesh—closed too tightly around her bones, but she hugged me back with surprising strength.

"We can never truly know another person," she said after we sat down. I thought I saw something move in the depths of her eyes, like an eel swimming through fathoms of green water.

"It's not that difficult," I said. "You spend time together."

Our tea was served. Hers was lavender and breath-of-hummingbird. "We are all essentially alone," she said.

"We don't have to be," I said. "That's why I'm here."

She wore a jacket hand-woven from the silk of milkweed trimmed in moss. When she sipped her tea, wisps of piney lavender and something that beat faster than the eye could see drifted my way.

"You don't understand," she said after a pause.

"I could if you explained." I took a deep swallow of my black tea with milk and honey.

"We are different," she said.

"Yes, but still within the realm of human. If we spend time together, we will get to know each other."

The food arrived. Her order was canapés of violet wrapped in rose petals, tied with fennel fronds. Mine was brown rice with stir-fried vegetables.

"Why not spend time with others?" she asked, spearing a canapé with a tiny glittering fork and cutting a piece the size of her pinky nail.

"Because we share blood and history," I said, heaping a forkful of rice and broccoli into my mouth.

"That is too close for me."

"You might get used to it," I said, filling my mouth again.

"I am not willing to change for you." She wafted the scent of her food toward herself and inhaled delicately.

"It took me twenty years to find your front door, and when you asked me to make an appointment, I did."

"I didn't ask you to my door. I didn't ask you to make an appointment. I just told you my requirements and you decided to accommodate."

"Yes," I said. "Will you ever accommodate me when I ask?"

"I will not change myself for anyone," she said, again. "It's not my job to meet your needs. It's your job."

"Will it always be this way?"

"Always."

That was the last I saw her. I have taken up residence at a house across the street where I watch others come and go from her labyrinth by appointment. The long, bare branches of her yew bushes twist like dancers in green shawls.

Sometimes, when I leave my house, I find a scarf tied to a low branch, a blend of blues and oranges, intricate as oil on water, or woven from butterfly wings frozen by winter come too soon. I know she's left the gift for me, so I wear it.

HITTING THE WALL

The first time Cassandra passed through the wall, she hadn't meant to. She had been standing at the edge of a retirement party at the hospital where she worked, feeling as uncomfortable as usual, when she leaned against the wall and fell right through.

The wall was still intact, but a gritty residue of plaster coated her tongue. The sour flavor was almost pleasant, and her internal organs felt scrubbed. If it hadn't been so wrong, it would have felt right. She spit the residue into a wastebasket and re-entered the party. No one had noticed she was gone.

She had always had boundary issues. The first time she heard the term was in her disastrous first marriage. "You're invading my boundaries," her then-husband shouted one snowy evening after they had been driving around screaming at each other for twenty minutes. They ended up in a cemetery.

"Boundaries?" she said, looking at the snow-covered tombstones that hunched under the high beams. "What are those?"

That marriage ended as quickly as it began.

She connected to people instantly, feeling the bitter peel and raw substance of them, wanting to skip the small talk and get to the core, because time was passing like a speeding bullet about to burst life's membrane. Sure, energy couldn't be destroyed, but once the body—that elaborate conduit of energy named Cassandra—died, the energy would disperse and become unrecognizable to itself.

Maybe this was why she also felt a keen separation from people. The phone rarely rang for her, nor did the text messages ping.

In fact, if it hadn't been for her second husband and their daughter, she would have been lonely. Together, the three of them lived in a bubble of paradise, feeding each other at dinner time with bare fingers.

Not surprisingly, neither her husband nor her daughter blinked that night when she shared with them that she had fallen through the wall earlier that day.

From then on, Cassandra began to pass through walls on purpose. She'd press herself against her friends' and colleagues' walls like soft cheese through a grater, and then she'd coalesce on the other side. They never saw her because people only see what they expect. She, on the other hand, saw more than she expected, a myriad of details that people weren't sharing. Usually, it was something small, like the fact that Deirdre, a stocky woman who had been her office mate of five years, who wore three-inch heels that made her calf muscles bulge, picked her nose when Cassandra was out of the office, or that the director of marketing had a leaky bladder and kept pads in the back of her desk drawer. Other times it was something momentous, like when Barbara, an admission clerk was quietly making burial arrangements for her husband, who had hanged himself. Yet Barbara had greeted her every day with the exact same smile.

Each time Cassandra passed through a wall, her organs felt sifted, but her feelings grew more and more clouded, not by what she discovered, but by the fact that so many people assiduously maintained such façades. She couldn't understand why.

"You might restrain yourself," her husband said with a smile at dinner one night, when she explained what she was doing. He wiped up the last of the hummus with a carrot stick and held it up to her mouth.

"But why?" she asked, letting him feed her.

He shrugged. "People like their privacy."

"But I've never bothered to cover my birthmark," she said, referring to the irregular wine-colored splotch on her left jawline. "If someone asked me how my day was, I'd tell them if it was crappy. Who is anyone kidding?"

"That's why we love you," her teenage daughter said, still in her bony stage, as she plucked a Concord grape from Cassandra's plate and squeezed it until it burst into her mouth.

After dinner, while watching TV, Cassandra braided and unbraided her daughter's hair, and her daughter, in turn, outlined her wine-colored birthmark with a blue ballpoint pen.

"It looks like a ruby-throated hummingbird, now," her daughter said, holding up a hand mirror. Cassandra looked at it distractedly. It did, indeed, look like a hummingbird, with its long beak probing the line of her jaw, wings reared along her cheek. She smiled, not looking at the rest of her face.

Sometimes, when she shared personal things with others, they called her brave. Cassandra rejected this assessment, except the day the topic of abortion came up in the cafeteria one lunch period. The most outspoken loudly proclaimed it murder. She felt compelled to admit she'd had an abortion at the end of her first marriage, and that even though she'd grieved the choice, she knew that giving up that fetus (and she used that word on purpose) had cleared the way to finding her second husband. Her daughter wouldn't exist without that sacrifice. Sharing this information had cost her a few heartbeats and a red face, but she wanted the silent among them to know that decent people made difficult choices.

When she told Deirdre this story, Deirdre gasped, pulling her chin back into her neck so that it formed a temporary double chin, and said, "Oh, I'd never do that." Caught off guard, Cassandra didn't ask if she meant the abortion or the admission of it. For a few weeks after that admission, when she passed people in the hall and made flickering eye contact with them, her smiles came out like grimaces, as she wondered if they'd heard the gossip about her and judged her. Nevertheless, she believed in the power of truth. The truth was supposed to set you free, after all, wasn't it?

One day, coming back from the X-ray department, rather than opening her office door with her key, Cassandra pressed herself through the wall. Deirdre hunched over her desk and whispered vehemently into the phone. "Why don't you touch me anymore? Is there someone else?" She had kicked her pumps off under her desk and tucked her feet around the base of her desk chair.

Cassandra stayed long enough to figure out that Deirdre was arguing with her husband and pressed herself back out. She waited a few minutes, then put the key to the lock. Deirdre, just hanging up the phone, turned to greet her brightly, her pumps now back on.

"How are you?" Cassandra asked.

"Fine," Deirdre said.

"How's the family?" Cassandra persisted.

After a fractional pause, Deirdre replied, "Jim just got us tickets to a Broadway show. Can't wait. How's your family?"

Cassandra leaned toward her for a second, ready to tell her what she had just done and seen, but the smooth expression on Deirdre's face bleached the intention out of her.

"Fine," Cassandra said, turning her face away, and sitting down to her computer screen.

All these discoveries would have been fine if she possessed verbal discretion. But one morning, her office mate answered her usual how-are-you with, "I'm a little tired, today."

Cassandra, unthinking, asked, "Are things any better with your husband?"

Deirdre stiffened. Her pupils constricted like a hermit crab pulling back into its shell. Then she averted her eyes and excused herself. Since that day, relations with Deirdre had been strained.

Another time in the cafeteria, in a conversation about fitness with the director of marketing, Cassandra took the opportunity to slip in that she'd heard that Kegel exercises could help with incontinence. The director ended their conversation gracefully, claiming she had just remembered an appointment. Cassandra couldn't tell if it was true or not.

Over time, it seemed that most of the people she knew avoided eye contact with her and kept their conversations shorter than usual, but she might have been imagining it. At night the closed circuit of her family's love still glowed in the surrounding darkness, but at work, she grew more and more angry.

Why didn't they like her? She had so much to give. She was kind, compassionate and nonjudgmental. In defiance, she continued to press herself through the walls, as if the more she did it, the more right it would be. But the weight of people's distrust and judgment, real or imagined, began to compact her.

Each time she pressed through a wall, it got harder to do, until finally one day, she pressed herself up against a wall and both her body and the wall remained solid. She drew back, ran her hand across its smooth surface, and tried again. No go.

After she stopped passing through walls, she found it easier to keep her thoughts to herself. Though her relationship with Deirdre never recovered, and the director of marketing still gave her only strained smiles, new friendships grew, like invasive weeds, easily plucked. The freedom this new kind of truth had brought her wasn't the kind she wanted. Maybe her husband was right, and it was only anxiety. Maybe she created the disconnection by a deeply internalized insecurity. Then again, maybe she saw a potential for something others rarely availed themselves of.

She and her family continued their orbit in a tiny sun-filled universe, and occasionally the phone rang for her and texts pinged, but they felt more like distractions than the deep connections she craved.

Sometimes at the end of the day at work, when the late afternoon sun slanted through her office window like an orange lozenge, she would touch the wall beside her desk and hunger for the sour prick of plaster on her tongue as if it was the only food left on earth.

SILVER LININGS

Numb as the inside of an urn, she listens while her teacher speaks. She pushes his words away the same way she twists the silver ring around her finger, away, and away, and away. Her throat aches with unwritten words. Devouring women, sympathetic ghouls, and towering flowers crowd her nightmares, but she doesn't know how to crack their code. What her body knows she doesn't know how to fit into the shapes of words.

His head floats high above his green glass lampshade. As he talks, he idly sifts and stirs her words, wrinkled, curled things she had managed to squeeze out. He flattens them on his leather desk pad and locks his fingers together to hold them down.

He says, "Some of your poems are okay, but your stories? Ugh. And what's with this poem?" He holds it up between thumb and forefinger. Together, in silence, they watch it squirm and lash like a worm pulled from soil.

The poem was about an old woman she had visited all semester in a nursing home, as part of a class on gerontology. The old woman tied a clock the size of a plate around her neck with cotton twine. Arthritis splayed her joints so she couldn't walk or knit. She was partially blind, so she couldn't read. Her hearing was bad, so she couldn't listen to recorded books, and her sixty-year-old son, her only child, died of cancer. "Why am I still alive?" she cried tearfully each time she visited. The girl didn't know what to say, so she wrote a poem wishing what no one dared to wish for this old woman.

"What are you, some kind of Nazi?" asks her teacher.

She can't see his eyes, the walls of his office, her words. All she sees is the plain silver ring she twists around and around her finger. Her throat feels hot and sore.

He tells her she should leave writing to someone else.

Pushing the ring around her finger cools her vocal cords, abraded by unspoken anguish. Her throat becomes a silver tube.

He sweeps his flattened hand through her throat and seals it shut. With both hands, he grasps her throat, and gingerly extracts a segment to form a perfect silver cup, the exact diameter of her unspoken words. He fills the cup with cool water and drinks, sighing contentedly.

She grips her ring so hard, she scratches herself. It flips into the air, flashing as it spins, and clatters to the floor, where it tilts into a crack between the wall and floor. She dives after it and somehow twists her body through the crack to follow.

On the other side, she lies in a wild wood. It is night. A boisterous creature prances faster than the speed of reason beyond a lace framework of trees, beckoning her to follow.

She is still chasing the creature today. Sometimes she zigzags through the woods until all thought expires. Other times, she becomes the creature, mute and distant as the stars, and just as eternal. She has met others in the woods, and after a chase, they sit in pewter dust at the edge, spinning rings to see what light they cast, reveling in the best part of humanity.

Once in a rare while, she stumbles into a clearing where her own words frost the ground like moonlight through leaves. Here, she discovers the words were never hers to begin with but inexact gifts from the mystery that temporarily soothed her throat when they showered the ground.

PRICE CHOPPER RESURRECTED

Every night men descend from the ceiling and veil the counters in plastic, then rearrange. In the morning the ketchup is on the other side of the aisle and the pesto is in the deli. The bakery is in the middle of the store instead of on the side, and the entrance is to the left. New walls have appeared. Old walls have disappeared.

Each morning Price Chopper resurrects itself differently. The center that was empty is now full of aisles stacked high with goods. The floors are now tiled more expensively than most of the customers' homes. Cash registers have been chopped and reincarnated into elegant check-out counters.

Employees don't know where to report, and dazed customers mill around, searching for their lost peanut butter and frozen fries. No one can remember what color the walls used to be, but now they are cantaloupe with red accents. The health food section has vanished. The soy milk has migrated to baking goods, and the dried peas are stacked in International.

Even the vegetables are stacked differently, beautifully, inside new black rectangles. Red leaf lettuce blooms vertically in a row below the green scallion paintbrushes and carrot exclamation marks.

What was merely large has become colossal. When in the dairy section one remembers the parsley, returning to the vegetable section gives one pause. It is so *far away... miles*. Senior citizens could power-walk the track-size perimeter every morning if paramedics could only be on call in the meat department.

Each day people adjust to the new arrangement. But the next morning, the milk has been removed to refrigerators along the edge, and the deli is now catty-corner. Or is it? No. It hasn't moved at all, everything around it has moved.

Where has the angel hair pasta gone? Where is the hummus? Why is the crumbled blue cheese in a refrigerator all by itself? How long has this gone on? The future is uncertain. A tiny old man hops in aisle five, trying to reach the towering chocolate milk mix that used to be at knee level. Someone help him!

People on endless quests open and close the doors of the quarter-mile refrigerators, rubber seals hugging and sucking in percussive bursts. Ah, the paralyzing splendor of abundance. The vertigo of one-stop shopping. Who knew that mark-ups could bear such inexhaustible fruit?

7

PIGEON LADY

What do I want most in the world?

I walk with my new husband and two socialite friends through Central Park. The fan-shaped ginkgo leaves have turned yellow and flutter down. The low, gray sky is beginning to let down water. My cold hands tangle in the holes of my coat pocket, a coat my husband has begged me to replace. It reflects badly on him, he says. I step ahead of them.

A ruffled explosion startles me, and I swivel to see a flock of pigeons burst into flight like a hundred sheets unfurled and snapping in stormwind. Angling straight for my head, they beat the air with feather and bone. I duck and turn, swirling out of my previous orbit. They cross over me, their destination the other bank, and descend slowly, whirring all around an old woman I had not seen standing there before, a woman whose hair is much too black, thick and long for her age, a woman who stands facing me with an enormous black plastic bag of crumbs. I cannot make out her eyes at that distance, only the thick kohl eye-liner, but her chin is up and she seems to be looking straight, not around, not up, or down at the pigeons framing her, but straight across, at me. For a second, with the pigeons graphing the air at even points from high to low, from deep to shallow, the woman is suspended in midair, like the Magritte painting of floating businessmen.

What I want most is for this woman whose figure has caused a riot of flapping wings, this woman whose face is deeply lined, whose orange-red lipstick stands out across the grays of late fall, I want this woman, whose arthritic hands pat a pigeon nestled in the hollow of her neck, under her frazzled, plastic black wig, this homeless woman, who must have picked the garbage for her bag of crumbs, or struck up an acquaintance with the cooks of certain restaurants.

I want this old woman to lift her eyes and say, I bless you.

8

DAPHNE RETURNS

Running, I became deer-light and lithe, springing over fallen logs through the forest, legs striking ground away from Apollo, from his shining face, from sunfire burning under my skin when he approaches, from dark wet urges, terrifying closeness, base smells. I flitted through the trees faster than moonlight. Yes! This was all I wanted, this here, now, loamy earth, scent of leaves, trees my only friends, the True Ones who serve without passion, who unite earth and sky unthinking, who never hate or hunger or dangle their crying prey between claws in curious delight. Trees give and take in equal measure, clean, sublime, stronger than hurricanes, anchored, yet pliant. Yes, I was right to run from Apollo.

Nevertheless, he caught me, his skin hot-surrounded me, scent of hay, of sweat, flash of white teeth, eyes burningest blue of the hottest day sky, his muscles musky golden felines across my back, voice surprisingly soft, purr of fire and lion. I twisted in his arms to get out but ended up facing that sweet concave at the base of his neck now drowning me. For just a second, I could have melted, could have tongue-to-saltness merged, following the blood down its dark tunnel into a world of flesh-eaters, baby-birthers and pollution. Father, save me!

Purity my power, I pushed him away from me, a cataract tumbling backward. Two steps and my thigh muscles woodened, my skin thickened, gray roughening to scale. My legs caught on each other, became one. Torso lengthened, arms shot skyward, muscles cramped as they twisted around bone becoming branch. Feet sprouted roots probed earth, swelled, pushed rock and soil aside, a grip of earth, a firm of firmament.

Barely could I feel his arms around me now, beating on my hardening trunk. His cries faded as my ears vanished. Pain drained as blood thinned and purified to sap, and with it, all of blood's dark messages of desire, envy, fear, love, and—hunger—most dangerous, devious, and confusing of all.

Replaced. By quiet, by orderly mineral messaging, a muttering of equations, a murmuring of measurements, equidistant and effervescing directions on how to sprout branches, how to turn sun to sugar with my fingers now leaves.

Language last to go. Human away the drain. What of all words their meaning from? Cambium green under bark, phloem and xylem coursing earth's ancient dictums newly clear, branchifying to sunfit. Downsink I to darkness most planetary, most still. Earth-pull-sky close and toxin translate to oxygen sweet. Slow. I no more, but allmind knowing and nowing, until only, sunhumming, I this.

9

LILITH CONFESSES

Yes, it's true, I swallowed Adam before I knew what I was doing. Didn't even see him go down.

He was such a whiner. Always complaining that I didn't want to serve him, that I wanted to be on top when we had sex.

So, he threw me out. That's when God made Eve.

But it was me Adam fantasized about in the placid waters of Eve's arms.

And, well, yes, I did run off with the arch-angel Samael. If you saw him, you wouldn't blame me. But after we did it, he claimed I had raped him with his own desire. So, I ate him too. Believe me, I saw what I was doing that time.

See that reddish-brown spot on the placemat?

That's all that's left of those two.

At least in my belly they can find their inner child.

WHAT BLOOMS

The only part of her first-grade teacher in Germany that she would remember was the flat of her hand, which slapped her face for fidgeting. The only memory that bloomed years later was how to sit in rows, feet firmly planted, hand tracing inky curlicues with a Pelican fountain pen.

In the family's third-story apartment, crouched under slanted ceilings, she and her brother pored over the German reader, *Struwwelpeter* illustrated in thick black ink filled in with orange and red.

The door flew open, and in he ran, the great, long, red-legg'd scissor-man.

Oh! Children, see! The tailor's come and caught out Little Suck-a-Thumb.

Snip, snip, snip, they go so fast, that both his thumbs were off at last.

Afterward, the thumbless boy, contrite, looked up at his mother, red beads of ink springing in two arches from the stumps of his thumbs.

"Ah, I knew he'd come," his mother said, *"to naughty little Suck-a-Thumb!"*

An ocean and a year later, back in America, sister and brother wandered far from the house, over bluestone sidewalks rumpled by the roots of towering maples, past houses where porches bulged like apron pockets filled with sweets. One day, they traipsed down a street they'd never taken before. There, beneath a blue house with gothic spires, a garden frothed. Lavender wands and orange suns pushed through spear-tipped iron pickets. Deep and airy as the sky, a language of flowers captured the children, emptied their minds, and filled their bodies with nothing but beauty, beauty, beauty.

A woman's head popped up from the flowers, hair black curly. She pointed her shears at them and said, "If you touch my flowers, I'll cut your ears off." *Snip, snip, snip, they rasped so loud, the shears of the dark-eyed garden frau.*

They stood long enough to imagine what those blades would do to their little pink ears. Then they ran back over broken slates, through bars of shadow, into their own dining room, where their grandmother ladled hot soup.

Many years later, the memory still blooms, bright and resistant to meaning.

CALLING DOWN THE MOUNTAIN

In memory of Tim Pantaleoni, 1962-1995

The mountain says nothing. It stands with its green heads wreathed in clouds. The ridge where his bike was found lunges upward to the King Kong wall, as we have dubbed it, the Ko'olau Range. Steam rolls up from the crevasses at the top like hair, keeping the peaks veiled until noon, or sometimes all day. The mountain walls are green and deeply cut like downward-grasping fingers. Pele pushed the mountain up. The violence is in the form. The mountain stands.

We who loved him stand at its foot looking up. We have flown five thousand miles to search for him. We shade our eyes. We pray. The mountain says nothing. The mountain is inviolable. We try to imagine which way he went. He might have gone straight up the sharp ridge, which climbs fast and narrows to a fin eight inches wide that brings us to our hands and knees over a two-hundred-foot drop. We who once encircled him twine ourselves along the

steep slope, wedging ourselves behind trunks to gain another
foothold, fighting through vines that strap us at waist and ankle.
Trees close to the wall of the mountain catch boulders the size of
curled bodies. Vining ferns cover the lower slopes. A body dropped
into them would be enveloped by five feet of springy growth. Even
the smell of human rot would not escape them. Orchids spread
their fragrance through the jungle; rose apples fall wantonly to the
ground. The mountain makes of us children, scaling its boney back.
The mountain is not an "it," as in an object, but neither is it male
nor female; it is larger than us; it is beyond us.

One minute he was fixing his landlady's door, the next minute
he was gone. He took nothing with him. He had come to the island
only six weeks before in a final attempt to begin a new life. He had
canoe practice that evening at 5:30. He was one of the only whites
ever allowed to join the native Hawaiian team.

After three days of absence, his landlady called his mother in
New York. His sister flew out. By the time she found his bike at the
foot of the trail, six days had passed. After a two-day search with
helicopters and dogs, the police called it off. No person who had
gone missing for more than 48 hours had ever been found on
Oahu.

We could never predict and now cannot retrodict the ways of
his mind. The possibilities of his mind are playful, quirky, rigid,
inventive. The possibilities of the mountain are greater. When we
put his mind, his monkey-tense arms and short quads, his furrowed
brow together with the mountain's jungle streams, rock walls and
guava groves, the possibilities multiply exponentially.

There are so many ways to die on the Ko'olau Range and, more
tantalizing, so many ways to keep on living if you are wounded,
between gentle daily rains, soothing temperatures, abundant rose
apples. As we comb the jungle, we eye broad ti-plant leaves for what
they might conceal. Impressions in the mud take the form of the
dead body we wish not to find.

He could be lying in a pool of water, just out of reach. Waterfalls spill between the knuckles of the mountain, forming pools, one fifty feet off the ground, and then again at one hundred. Perhaps he scaled a waterfall too high for us. We push hard against the out-thrust hands of the mountain that seem to say, "Halt, lest you be prepared to follow him all the way." The rock walls are sheathed in slippery algae. When we teeter on the rocky lips we have conquered out of sheer desperation, we feel, suddenly, how our heads would burst like gourds on the rocks below. The pool before us is empty. We cannot follow him over the next wall to the pool just beyond.

Gravity on the mountain is reversed. Rather than pulling us down, it pulls us up, raking us over its boulders and fallen trees into its heart, with the promise that he is just beyond reach. As hard as we struggle physically to go up, we struggle harder emotionally to go back down. Each night we limp to bed, muddy, bruised, and empty-handed.

When we are not scouring the mountain, we scour his letters and our memories. Was it an accident? Or had he been walking toward this conclusion his whole life long?

In his second to last letter he wrote:

Have had several half-experiences on this trip, wonderful hikes and appreciation of natural beauties, and some good exchanges with people that do not feel complete somehow. Then I'll tell a story about it—and the telling seems to fill the cup to the brim after the fact. I feel a bit as though I'm lying to my listener, portraying the experience as one that held my interest—whereas the main feature of most of these experiences is their emptiness—the spirit-confounding flatness of beauties and complexities that seem as though they ought to be sufficient but are not. They do not nourish me. I am half-starved in the wilderness.

He was thirty-three, the age Christ was when he was crucified. Was it just coincidence, or an unconscious resonance that he wrote in his last letter:

> When I read the Bible, Jesus seems to be saying, "Close the book, man! Stop reading, and start living!" And the telling of his story, the unceasing recording and re-recording of his actions seems an astonishing lack of faith on the part of his would-be followers, a spiritual opacity that would enrage their idol could he witness it: a man, completely awake, attempting to wake others. They manage to get their eyelids open but cannot get out of bed.
>
> In my own case, I feel fooled into believing that somehow, if you study math and science hard enough—with enough magic—then you will have adventures—as if A can lead to B. I think this is false, and wonder if those stories are told precisely because it never really happens. More to the point, I suppose, is that if you study A very hard, life starts to look very much like A itself—you start to see things in terms of the language you know well—thereby closing out all of the experience that lies outside your known realm—which of course is most experience.

When white light, such as sunlight, enters a glass prism, out of the other side comes not white light, but all colors from deep red, to orange, yellow, green, blue and violet. Such was the light of his smile. Tines of light leapt in his flat-lidded eyes that only seconds before stared as detached as a lizard. His lips were full, his neck taut, his voice low and resonant as a cello. He formed his words deliberately and spoke with the cadence of a bass drum.

His skin was smooth and hairless, and every muscle of his body was cleanly shaped by the hours he spent trying to live each moment of his life fully, by running, climbing, and swinging on monkey bars to the delight of children who gathered to watch him in the park at dusk. But his thoughts formed a strangling pattern that kept him fixed and lifeless no matter how much he swung from the rafters, or danced the samba, or laughed. And he did all these things, more than most people in a lifetime.

Standing on that tangled red trail, halfway up the mountain, overlooking two bays on an island far out in the dark blue Pacific, we are enacting the metaphor for his life: he is both alive and dead, all around us and nowhere; we are trying to rescue him from his path, and we cannot. Perhaps we should not. Because we don't know the whole story. We never will.

In our minds he dies a thousand deaths: he falls and breaks his legs, and crawls under a rock ledge before he faints, he hits his head and is delirious, lying face to sky, hearing footsteps pass him by, but cannot wake up enough to call out. Perhaps he is not quite dead when the wild pigs, invisible to us but for their cloven tracks and low dens, approach him; or emerging from the jungle into a cannabis field, he sees the gun in a stranger's hand and his entire life force swells behind his sternum to shield off the bullet that, in a flash, pops his skin and reveals him to be just the bag of blood we all carry on our bones.

Or this: he is climbing the King Kong wall without ropes and when he reaches the top, he turns around, faces the sea, and for the first time in his life stops thinking, raises his head, and simply lets go.

However it occurred, perhaps the moment when he fell was the shortest distance between himself and life, which he had searched for all his life.

Time is slow. If he is still alive, his life is leaving him. We who listened to him all our lives wrap rocks in ti-plant leaves as offerings to the mountain. But six days turn into twelve and twelve to twenty-four. We cannot find him. He has disappeared from the earth, leaving no trace. Or disappeared into the earth. His parts may be dispersed into the sun, the air, the bellies of pigs, the shining leaves of trees. The mountain may have swallowed him; the mountain may hold him tight to its breast.

We stand at the foot of the Ko'olau Range, shading our eyes, looking up. The mountain holds secrets high in its peaks, in hidden valleys that no one can reach except a strange eccentric, strong man, driven by the desire to fully live for one minute—to be released from the self-entrapping circles of his mind. Prayer circles are said to be hidden here, that only natives know, with animals painted in red and black upon the walls. Dancing warriors are said to emerge at night. They are tall as the mountain; they stand straight as rain, raise knees in jagged forms, carry spears, move in slanted lines across the night, stamp bare feet upon the earth until the mouths of stones open wide.

We, the living, sometimes smoke, or sleep or drink to dull or enhance ourselves, or break down and weep, because we cannot live each moment fully as he thought we should, as he died trying to do. It is too much for our finite minds and hearts.

I try to understand what has become of him or why. Did he try too hard to taste the atom of which we are made? Because definition never worked, seeking as it does to pin life down and fix it, I tell stories to try to make sense of it—stories to encompass it, stories to set it back in motion, so that I may keep myself spinning within the spinning fact of our existence. Stories such as this:

Voices are babbling and churning like water over stones. He awakes to find the river is his own voice, a new knowing, blown over vocal cords into sound: The energy which holds atoms together is akin to human joy. Atoms stand before him, bright as giant stars in a black sky, but close enough to touch. Though he cannot move, he leaps, and the atoms part, spinning past him to either side as he enters.

We are bodies in motion. Organic patterns of energy, stepping uniquely in a dance we know only partially in some minuscule way. We go back to the mainland, kneel in the bathtub and feel the warm water on our thighs, thinking, "He will never feel this again." We make food, cut and hang Sheetrock, and must somehow accept the unfathomable that lies between these acts. Within these acts. We must somehow incorporate a design as simple and mysterious as the roots that begin to grow from a section of dead ti-plant left lying on damp ground, for we are bodies in motion, in beauty, in terror, in motion.

The mountain stands. And we stand, not understanding what stands between us. All this, of which we are made, an absolute physical fact, with the unknown unfolding from it like the clouds rolling up from the peaks, like smoldering Pele, bathed in red, petal-thin silk, ribbons of glass hair undulating above her.

We pray that the mountain became a prism for his white light. But the mountain is what it is. We stand. The mountain stands. We shade our eyes. We pray.

WORLD'S END

We gave up hope, and the world came to an end. Dark clouds beat the sky, lightning split the air, and thunder rolled down like cannon shot. Winds flattened the black grass and threatened to blow us away. We chopped down the last tree on the earth we had loved so much and crawled under its bare branches so that each branch pinned us down.

After a few hours like this, a leader among us emerged. He crawled out from one of the branches, and even though the wind lashed his long hair against his jaw, he waved for us to follow. The contours of his face spelled something we couldn't name, and we mustered enough courage to follow him. He led us to a cave.

Deep underground, a river flowed so slowly that the surface shone like obsidian. Linked flat-bottomed boats drifted downriver. He climbed into one and we climbed in after him, nestling around him like chicks around a dove. We drifted in silence scanning the cave's torchlit roof for cracks. When thunder detonated overhead and shook the ground, we inched closer, raising a cloud of warmth with our feathery touches.

He fell into an exhausted sleep. We drifted on in silence. As we wound our way through the darkness, our consciences began to blister. We had not been the direct cause of the earth's destruction, but we had not done all we could to stop it. We had continued to drink its milk and honey, and had done little but lay waste to it. We had taken more than we gave.

A shockwave of air exploded overhead, louder than before. We shook our leader's knee and called his name. He did not wake. The torches burned low and the air yielded less and less to breathe. We stroked his beloved hands and face, but in the darkness, they grew hard and cold. The torches flared and revealed that his face had turned to bone. We recoiled from his empty sockets and loose teeth.

The boat drifted, and our fear ballooned, filling the darkness. Some began to lament, while others, barely restraining the urge to beat the fearful ones into silence, grit their teeth.

Just when darkness was about to tear our minds apart, someone reached out, tentatively, and stroked our leader's skull. Others leaned forward and rubbed his finger bones between theirs. Still, others stroked his femur, and thus we drifted through the darkest part of our night.

Eventually, the torches re-ignited, and the air became breathable. New flesh bathed our leader's face, and blood pumped radiantly through his body. The tunnel opened into a broad cavern that opened to the sky. Relief fell open like a sleeper's palm, and we burst into laughter. The storm was over.

Our leader woke briefly and said we should make gifts for each other. We had only bits of rag and a few loose threads, but we fashioned them into rings and necklaces and adorned each other. He told us we didn't need him anymore and went back to sleep.

Talking and laughing, we stepped out of the boats and out of the cave, ready to start the world again.

THE SPIRAL STAIRCASE

The spiral stair is formed by an ellipsis of such elegant geometry that it permits only movement. On its wooden steps, worn to shallow basins, and within its rising banister, inertia is impossible. At certain points, the staircase spins off landings, at other points, rooms.

1. Nautilus

The young woman dreams always of chambers that lead to other chambers. Each chamber has several doors, and each door leads to another chamber with more doors. Sometimes she can see through one chamber into the next and the next, with complete disregard for the walls, as though she were looking down the corridor of infinity in a mirror's reflection of itself. In the dreams, she knows that each room has a purpose, an obvious purpose, and yet she has no idea what it is. Each room differs from the others in only one aspect: the orientation might have shifted, the walls might be marked, or the light might fall at a different angle; otherwise, they are identical. She wanders from room to room, trying, again and again, to understand what makes one room completely different from another while remaining exactly the same. The monotony of endless differentiation exhausts her eyes and makes her dizzy; her very consciousness vaporizes, and her blood turns white.

In the dreams, the fact that she ought to know the purpose of each room, and the fact that she doesn't know, weighs on her. Each chamber seems the ante-chamber to the next. Each room leads her on, hinting always at the knowledge just within reach if she were only to go a little farther. Each time, she is filled with great expectation. Each time she is met with disappointment. Gradually the torment grows to such a feverish pitch that she wakes up.

Sometimes she doesn't enter the rooms. They don't have doors; they just lead into each other without opening or closing. Sometimes it is merely the knowledge of their existence beyond the wall, going on forever and ever, having everything and nothing to do with each other, that oppresses her.

Sometimes she hears voices from another room. She thinks she does. She cannot tell. The sound is so faint it teases her ear. Sometimes it is a faint knocking, as though someone very far away were trying to get in—or out. Other times, she thinks she hears footsteps—or laughter—or crying. She cannot discern. She strains so hard to hear that her ears fill with silence.

She wants to stop wanting to know. But even as she is promising herself that she will stop, she finds herself looking one last time, and then another last time.

Once she entered a chamber and felt quite distinctly that someone had just left. She tried quickly to follow. She caught a glimpse of a person just slipping into the chamber beyond. It is just a flicker, a flash of white, a hand disappearing from the door frame. But in the next room she found only the presence of departure, and in the next, a trace of absence.

2. Carousel

The horizon ascends to eclipse the sun. Darkness descends, sucking up lengthened shadows as it goes, robbing objects of their substance. Molecules seeth fierce and casual as rising steam before our very eyes. We pay no mind. Everything passes as nothing at a moment's notice.

And across the way through a window, a light goes on. An old man passes in and out of sight. Something other than time has worn his face gray. The light goes out.

Voices from another room rise; a child is crying; a door is slammed; feet clatter on the stairs. All unseen.

The old man shuffles from room to room, stopping here and there as if intention had escaped him, and he is waiting for it to return. He isn't searching; he knows what he will find. Something stronger than gravity pulls him down, something fragile about the shoulders, something beautiful about the mouth. In his hands, once stiff with muscle, now hammocks of skin between bones, he carries something, gently.

Someone is dancing to the radio, different voices mingle in different rooms, separate conversations spawning unknown resonations, each room another setting for another scene in a different play, rooms stacked on top of each other going on and on indefinitely. (How is it that we live what we can never apprehend?)

And still, across the way, a light goes on. The old man passes in and out of sight. In his hands—a picture which he moves from wall to wall, now here, now there. Light goes out.

3. The Landing

He jumps into the car, turns it on, and starts. Then he jumps into the car, turns it on, and starts. Then he

4. Paradise

The room is almost dark, and in the darkness, bare wood floors glow gently as bones do. Windows line a wide expanse of floor. Gray light sifts through the windows and renders the meeting of wall to floor vague. The room is empty. A very old woman sits in the center. Nothing in the room but the old woman. A large oval box sits on her lap. The woman and the box. Behind her, a picture frame hangs on the wall with nothing in it. The woman, the box, and the empty frame. She has had the box all her life. It belonged to her mother, and before that, her mother's mother, and so on, for generations. It is dear to her.

No one knows what is in it, the box. No one has ever looked inside. Nothing in the box. It feels empty. It could be empty for all she knows, but she doesn't look. What does she know? She wants to know, but she never looks.

She sits, face raised upon the half-light, stroking the box while threads as delicate as nothing fall across her face, binding even as they break.

ACKNOWLEDGMENTS

"The Opal Maker" was published in *The Collagist*; "Daphne Returns," formerly "Ending Hunger," was published in *Gone Lawn*; "Pigeon Lady" was published in *Artists Unite*; "My Sister's Labyrinth" was published in *Eclectica Magazine*; "Divorce in a Different Light" was published in *The Times Union*; "The Spiral Staircase" was published in *The North American Review*; and "Price Chopper Resurrected" was published in *The Saratogian*.

ABOUT THE AUTHOR

Lâle Davidson's stories have appeared in *The North American Review*, *The Collagist*, *Fickle Muse*, and *Big Lucks*, among others. Roxane Gay selected "The Opal Maker" as one of The Wigleaf Top 50 Very Short Fictions of 2015. *Strange Appetites* won The Adirondack Center for Writers People's Choice Award of 2018.

She has taught writing and public speaking for nearly thirty years at SUNY Adirondack, and lives in a stone-arched, ivy-covered house in Saratoga Springs, NY with her husband and way too many cats.

Winner of the Adirondack Center for Writing's
People's Choice Award 2016

During heart surgery on a woman, the doctor discovers her sister tucked inside. She doesn't want to come out. A woman traverses boundaries, even walls. By turns surreal, mournful, and droll, this collection of short stories investigates our conflicting urge for intimacy and transcendence.

Enter this cabinet of wonders to find your mind and spirit expand. While the concerns and struggles are familiar — loneliness, troubled marriages, envy, hungers of various sorts —these fabulist tales shed fresh light, producing strange and tasty blooms.
~Ron MacLean, author of *We Might as Well Light Something on Fire*

The places her metaphors take us are intimate and quiet—the damp space under stones, the mushrooms that grow in forests.
~Dana Diehl, editor of *The Collagist*

Made in United States
North Haven, CT
30 October 2021